Contents

The Fairy Cow

By Jeremiah Curtin

In the parish of Drummor lived a farmer called Tom Connors. He had some land, four cows, a wife and five children.

Connors had one cow that was better than the other three, and she went by the name of Cooby. On one corner of Connors' farm there was a fairy fort, and the cow Cooby used to go into the fort, but Connors always drove her out, and told his wife and boys to keep her away from the fort.

Rapunzel

and other stories

Miles Kelly

First published in 2011 by Miles Kelly Publishing Ltd
Harding's Barn, Bardfield End Green, Thaxted, Essex, CM6 3PX, UK

2 4 6 8 10 9 7 5 3 1

Publishing Director Belinda Gallagher

Creative Director Jo Cowan

Editor Amanda Askew

Senior Designer Joe Jones

Designer Kayleigh Allen

Production Manager Elizabeth Collins

Reprographics Anthony Cambray, Stephan Davis, Jennifer Hunt

ISBN 978-1-84810-443-3

Printed in China

British Library Cataloguing-in-Publication Data
A catalogue record for this book is available from the British Library

ACKNOWLEDGEMENTS
Artworks are from the Miles Kelly Artwork Bank

Made with paper from a sustainable forest

www.mileskelly.net
info@mileskelly.net

www.factsforprojects.com

Self-publish your
children's book

buddingpress.co.uk

One morning when Connors went to drive his cows home to be milked he found Cooby in the field with her legs broken. He killed the cow that minute for the family to eat.

One morning after Tom was gone to the bog to cut turf, his wife went out to milk their remaining cows, and what should she see but a cow walking into the fort that looked just like Cooby. Soon the cow came out, and with her a girl.

"Oh, then," said Mrs Connors, "I'd swear that is Cooby, if we hadn't eaten her."

The girl milked the cow, and then cow and girl disappeared. The following day Tom's

wife went to milk again, and again she saw the cow go into the fort, and the girl come out to milk it.

'God knows 'tis the very cow. I'll tell Tom tonight, and he may do what he likes,' she thought.

When Connors came home in the evening, his wife said, "You remember Cooby?"

"Why shouldn't I remember Cooby, after eating most of her?"

"Indeed then, Tom, I saw Cooby today, inside the fort with a girl milking her."

"Well, I'll go in the morning, and if it's our Cooby I'll bring her home with me," said Tom, "Even if all the devils in the fort are before me."

Early in the morning Tom started across his land, and never stopped till he came to the fort, and there, he saw the cow walking in through the gap to the fort, and he knew her that minute.

"'Tis my cow Cooby," said Connors, "and I'll

have her. I'd like to see the man who would keep her from me."

That minute the girl came out with her pail and stool and walked towards Cooby.

"Stop where you are – don't milk that cow!" cried Connors.

"Let the cow go," said Tom, "this is my cow. Go to your master and tell him to come out to me."

The girl went inside the fort and disappeared, but soon a fine-looking young man came and spoke to Connors. "What are you doing here, my man," asked he, "and why did you stop my servant from milking the cow?"

"She is my cow," said Tom, "and by that same token I'll keep her."

"But I've had this cow a long time. And didn't you eat your own cow?"

"I don't care what cow I ate," said Tom. "I'll have

this cow, for she is my Cooby."

They argued and argued. Tom declared that he'd take the cow home. "And if you try to prevent me," said he to the man, "I'll tear the fort to pieces."

"Indeed, then, you'll not tear the fort."

Tom got so vexed that he made as though to fight the man. The man ran and Tom after him into the fort. When Tom was inside, he forgot all about fighting. He saw many people dancing and enjoying themselves, and he thought, 'Why shouldn't I do that myself?' With that he went up to a fine-looking girl, and, taking her out to dance, told the piper to strike up a hornpipe.

The young man came up and said, "Well, you are a brave man and courageous, and for the future we'll be good friends. You can take the cow."

"I will not take her, you may keep her, for you

are all very good people."

"Well," said the young man, "the cow is yours, and it's why I took her because there were many children in the fort without nurses, but the children are reared now, and you may take the cow. I put an old stray horse in place of her and made him look like your own beast, and it's an old horse you've been eating all the year. From this day forwards you'll grow rich and have luck. We'll not trouble you, but help you."

Tom took the cow and drove her home. From that day forwards Tom Connors' cows had two calves apiece and his mare had two foals and his sheep two lambs every year. Every acre of his land gave him as much crop in one year as another man got in seven years. At last Connors was a very rich man – and why not, when the fairies were with him?

Paddy Corcoran's Wife

By William Carleton

Paddy Corcoran's wife was for several years afflicted with a kind of complaint that nobody could properly understand. She was sick, and she was not sick, she was well, and she was not well, she was as ladies wish to be who love their lords, and she was not as such ladies wish to be. In fact nobody could tell what the matter with her was. The poor woman was delicate beyond belief, and had no appetite at all.

She lay bedridden, trying doctors of all sorts and sizes, and all without a farthing's benefit, until, at the long run, poor Paddy was nearly brought to despair.

Then one harvest day, as she lay moaning about her hard condition, on her bed by the kitchen fire, a little woman dressed in a neat red cloak came in, and sitting down by the hearth, said, "Well, Kitty Corcoran, you've had a long lie of it there on the broad of yer back for seven years, and you're just as far from being cured as ever."

"Ay" said the other, "in truth that's what I was this minute thinking of."

"It's yer own fault, then," says the little woman.

"Ah, how is that?" asked Kitty, "sure I wouldn't be here if I could help it? Do you think it's a pleasure to me to be sick and bedridden?"

"No," said the other, "I do not — but I'll tell you

the truth – for the last seven years you have been annoying us. I'm here to let you know the reason why you've been sick so long as you are. For all the time you've been ill, your children have thrown out yer dirty water after dusk and before sunrise, at the very time we're passing yer door, which we pass twice a day. Now, if you avoid this and throw it out in a different place, at a different time, the sickness will leave you and you'll be as well as ever you were." She then bade her goodbye, and disappeared.

Kitty immediately did as she was asked, and the next day she found herself in good health once more.

The Three Wishes

An English folk tale

There was once a poor fisherman who lived by the sea in a tumbledown old cottage. He lived with his wife, who was always grumbling no matter how hard the fisherman worked.

One evening he threw the nets out for one last try before it grew dark. He had caught nothing all day. As he began pulling the nets in, the fisherman's hopes rose – the nets were heavy. But when he hauled them in, there was only one tiny

fish lying at the bottom. Then the fish spoke. The fisherman rubbed his eyes in astonishment.

"Please throw me back," said the fish. "I am so small I would not make much of a meal for you."

But the fisherman was tired and hungry.

"Even though you are small I cannot throw you back. My wife would not be pleased if I came home empty-handed." he said with a deep sigh.

"I will grant you the first three wishes made in your cottage if you let me go," said the fish, "but I should warn you that wishes do not always give you what you really want."

Well, the fisherman did not hear the fish's warning. All he heard was the bit about three wishes, and he thought that finally his grumbling wife could have whatever she wanted. So he carefully untangled the tiny fish from the nets and placed it back in the sea. With a flick of its tail the fish disappeared deep, deep under water.

The fisherman ran home and told her all about the tiny fish. But instead of being pleased, she just shouted at him as usual.

"Trust you to believe such a thing! Whoever heard of a talking fish. You must be daft," and she slammed down a plate of dry bread and a rind of cheese in front of the poor fisherman.

"I wish this was a plate of fine sausages, I am so hungry," said the fisherman wistfully.

No sooner were the words out of his mouth than there was a wonderful smell and there in front of

him was a plate of sizzling sausages! He was delighted and reached for his knife when his wife yelled at him,

"Why couldn't you have wished for something better? We could have had chests of gold and fine clothes to wear!" and this from the woman who had refused to believe his story only a few moments before. "You stupid fool! I wish the sausages were at the end of your nose!"

There was a ghastly silence as the wife looked at her poor husband. Hanging from the end of his nose was a great string of sausages. The fisherman remembered what the fish had said – the first three wishes made in the cottage.

The Three Wishes

The fisherman and his wife pulled at the sausages, but they were stuck . There was nothing for it, they would have to use the last wish.

"I wish the sausages would disappear," said the fisherman sadly, and they did in a flash. So there they sat, the poor fisherman and his grumbling wife. No delicious supper of sizzling sausages and, much worse, no magic wishes. The fisherman never caught the tiny fish again, and his wife never stopped grumbling. Wishes do not always give you what you really want!

The Mermaid of Zennor

A Cornish legend

The bell was ringing, calling the villagers of Zennor to Sunday service. It was a simple little granite towered church, built to withstand the wild winds that could roll in from the sea. Matthew stood in the choir stalls and looked at the new bench he had been carving. It was nearly finished and wanted only one more panel to be carved.

As the voices of the congregation rang out in the hymns, a sweet, pure voice was heard. A voice that

no one had heard before. When the villagers turned to leave at the end of the service, there at the back of the little church stood the most beautiful woman any of them had ever seen. Her dress was made of silk, at one moment green, the next blue, like the sea. Round her neck she wore a gleaming necklace of pearls, and her golden hair fell down her back almost to the floor.

As Matthew walked out, the woman placed her hand on his sleeve.

"Your carving is beautiful, Matthew."

Matthew blushed and turned his rough cap round and round in his great red hands.

"Why, thank you ma'am," he managed to stutter before he fled out of the church. Where the beautiful lady went no one quite saw.

The next day Matthew was hard at work, carving the decoration of leaves that went round

the edge of the bench when he heard the soft rustle of silk. There stood the woman again.

"What will you put in the last panel, Matthew?" she whispered. Matthew sensed a strong smell of the sea in the tiny church as he bent to get up off his knees but when he looked up again, there was no sign of the woman.

The next Sunday the lady was in church again. She looked deep into Matthew's eyes as she sang the hymns, and when he walked slowly out, she was waiting for him.

"Will you carve my image in the last panel, Matthew?" she asked and her voice was gentle. Matthew's deep blue eyes gazed far over her head, out towards the sea, but he did not reply. Only the schoolmaster and his wife noticed that the seat where the woman had sat was wet with sea water.

Time passed, and every Sunday the woman

came to church. Matthew seemed like a man in a dream, his eyes always looking out to sea. The final panel was still not finished on the bench. November came, and with it the mist curled up from the sea. Night after night a light was to be seen late in the church. The gentle sound of wood chipping drifted out with the mist, but no one ventured into the church.

It was the parson who discovered the finished bench when he went in to open up the church one morning. The church floor was wet with sea water. The stub of a candle stood among a great pile of wood shavings on the floor. The final panel of the bench was the best Matthew had

ever carved. It was a mermaid, long hair falling down her back, the scales of her great fish tail in deep relief. She looked almost alive.

Matthew had not slept in his bed that night, nor was he ever seen again in Zennor. The mysterious woman never came to church again. The schoolmaster and his wife never talked of the wet seat. Only the fishermen would shake their heads as they sat talking on the winter's evenings. They would talk of the mermaid they had seen off the coast, and of the young man with the deep blue eyes who was always swimming by her side.

Pandora's Box

A Greek myth

When the world was first created, it was a happy place of light and laughter; there was no such thing as sadness or pain. The sun shone every day and the gods came down from heaven to walk and talk with the humans.

One afternoon, a man called Epimetheus and his wife, Pandora, were outside tending their flower garden when they saw the god Mercury approaching. He was bowed down by a dark

wooden chest that he was carrying on his shoulders. Pandora rushed to get the god a drink, while Epimetheus helped him lower the chest to the ground. It was tied shut with golden cords and was carved with strange markings.

"My friends, would you do me a great favour?" sighed Mercury. "It is so hot and the box is so heavy! May I leave it here for a while?"

"Of course you can," smiled Epimetheus.

The man and the god heaved the chest indoors.

"Are you sure that no one will find it?" asked Mercury anxiously. "NO ONE under ANY circumstances must open the box."

"Don't worry," laughed Epimetheus and Pandora, and they waved goodbye to the god.

All of a sudden, Pandora stopped still and frowned. "Listen, Epimetheus!" she hissed. "I am sure I heard someone whispering our names!"

Epimetheus and Pandora listened hard. At first, they heard nothing but the twittering of the birds. Then, they heard the distant sound of their names being called from outside.

"It's our friends!" cried Epimetheus, happily.

But Pandora looked puzzled and shook her head. "No, Epimetheus, those aren't the voices I heard," she said, firmly.

"They must have been!" Epimetheus laughed. "Come on now, let's go and see everyone."

"I'd rather stay here for a while," Pandora insisted.

As soon as Epimetheus was gone, Pandora hurried over to the strange box and waited. After only a few seconds, she heard it again — distant voices calling "Pandora!" The voices were so low and whispery that Pandora wasn't sure whether she really was hearing them or was just imagining

it. She bent down closer and put her ear to the lid. No, she was sure. The box was calling to her!

"Let us out, Pandora! We are trapped in here in the darkness! Please help us to escape!"

Pandora jumped back with a start. Mercury had expressly forbade anyone to open the box... and yet the voices sounded so sad and pitiful.

"Pandora!" they came again. "Help us!"

Pandora could stand it no longer. Hurriedly, she knelt down and worked at the tight golden knots. All the time, the whispering and pleading voices filled her ears. At last the knots were undone and the gleaming cords fell away. She took a deep breath and opened the lid.

At once, Pandora realized she had done a terrible thing. The box had been crammed with all the evils in the world – thousands of tiny moth-like

creatures that stung people with their wings and caused hurt and misery wherever they went. Now, thanks to Pandora, the evils were free! They flew up out of the chest in a great swarm and fluttered all over Pandora's skin. For the very first time, Pandora felt pain and regret. She began to wail with despair, and all too late, she slammed the lid back down onto the box.

Outside, Epimetheus heard his wife's cries and came running as fast as he could. The creatures fluttered to sting and bite him, before speeding off through the window into the world beyond. For the first time ever, Epimetheus began to shout at his wife in anger. Pandora yelled back, and the couple realized in horror that they were arguing.

"Let me out!" interrupted a high voice. Pandora and Epimetheus grabbed onto each other in a panic. The voice was coming from inside the box.

"Don't be afraid of me! Let me out and I can help you!" came the voice.

"What do you think?" Pandora whispered to Epimetheus, wide-eyed.

"Surely you can't do any more mischief than you already have done," he grumbled. So Pandora shut her eyes and opened Mercury's chest for a second time.

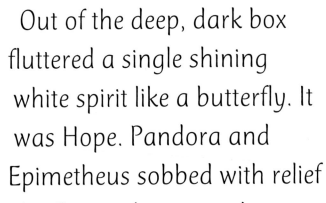

Out of the deep, dark box fluttered a single shining white spirit like a butterfly. It was Hope. Pandora and Epimetheus sobbed with relief as she fluttered against their skin and soothed their stinging wounds. Then she was gone, darting out of the window and into the world after the evils. And luckily, Hope has stayed with us ever since.

Rapunzel

By the Brothers Grimm

Once upon a time there lived a man and his wife who for years and years had wanted a child. One day the wife was looking sadly out of the window. Winter was coming but in the garden next door, which was surrounded by a huge great wall, she could just see rows and rows of delicious vegetables. In particular, she could see a huge bunch of rapunzel, a special kind of lettuce. Her mouth watered, it looked so fresh and green.

"Husband, I shall not rest until I have some of that rapunzel growing next door," she whispered.

The husband clambered over the wall and quickly picked a small bunch, which he took back to his wife. She made it into a salad, and ate it all up. But the next day, all she could think of was how delicious it had been so she asked him to pick her some more.

He clambered over the wall, and was picking a small bunch of the rapunzel when a voice behind him hissed, "So you are the one who has been stealing my rapunzel!"

When he spun round, there stood a witch and she looked very angry indeed. The husband was terrified, but he tried to explain that his wife had been desperate for some fresh leaves for her salad.

"You may take all the leaves you require then, but you must give me your first child when she is

born," smiled the witch, and it was not a nice smile. The husband was greatly relieved, however, for he knew that there was little chance of his wife ever having a daughter so he fled back over the wall, clutching the bunch of rapunzel. He did not tell his wife of his meeting with the witch for he thought it would only frighten her, and he soon forgot all about his adventure.

But it all came back to him when nine months later his wife gave birth to a beautiful baby girl. No sooner had she laid the baby in her cradle, than the witch appeared to claim the child. The wife wept, the husband pleaded but nothing could persuade the witch to forget the husband's awful promise, and so she took the tiny baby away.

The witch called the baby Rapunzel. She grew into a beautiful girl with long, long hair as fine as spun gold. When she was sixteen, the witch took Rapunzel and locked her in a tall tower so no one would see how beautiful she was. The witch threw away the key to the tower, and so whenever she wanted to visit Rapunzel she would call out, "Rapunzel, Rapunzel, let down your hair." Rapunzel would then throw her golden plait of hair out of the window at the top of the tower so the witch could slowly scramble up.

Now one day, a handsome young prince was riding through the woods. He heard the witch call out to Rapunzel and he watched her climb up the tower. After the witch had gone, the prince came to the bottom of the tower and he called up,

"Rapunzel, Rapunzel, let down your hair," and he climbed quickly up the shining golden plait. You can imagine Rapunzel's astonishment when she saw the handsome prince standing in front of her but she was soon laughing at his stories. When he left, he promised to come again the next day, and he did. And the next, and the next, and soon they had fallen in love with each other.

One day as the witch clambered up Rapunzel exclaimed, "You are slow! The prince doesn't take nearly as long to climb up the tower," but no sooner were the words out of her mouth than she realized her terrible mistake. The witch seized the long, long golden plait and cut it off. She drove Rapunzel far, far away from the tower, and then sat down to await the prince. When the witch heard him calling, she threw the golden plait out of the window. Imagine the prince's dismay when he sprang into the room only to discover the horrible witch instead of his beautiful Rapunzel! When the witch told him he would never see his Rapunzel again, in his grief he flung himself out of the tower. He fell into some brambles, which scratched his eyes so he could no longer see.

And thus he wandered the land, always asking if anyone had seen his Rapunzel. After seven long

years, he came to the place where she had hidden herself away. As he stumbled down the road, Rapunzel recognized him and with a great cry of joy she ran up to him and took him gently by the hand to her little cottage in the woods. As she washed his face, two of her tears fell on the prince's eyes and his sight came back. And so they went back to his palace and lived happily ever after. The witch, you will be pleased to hear, had not been able to get down from the tower, so she did NOT live happily ever after!

The Fairy Blackstick

From *The Rose and the Ring*
by William Makepeace Thackeray

Between the kingdoms of Paflagonia and Crim Tartary, there lived a mysterious person, who was known as the Fairy Blackstick, after the ebony wand that she carried.

When she was young, and had been first taught the art of conjuring by her father, she was always practising her skill, whizzing about from one kingdom to another upon her black stick. She had turned numberless wicked people into beasts,

birds, millstones, clocks, pumps, boot jacks, umbrellas, or other absurd shapes, and, in a word, was one of the most active of the whole College of Fairies.

But after two or three thousand years of this sport, I suppose Blackstick grew tired of it. Or perhaps she thought, 'What good am I doing by sending this princess to sleep for a hundred years? By fixing a black pudding on to that fool's nose? By causing diamonds and pearls to drop from one little girl's mouth, and vipers and toads from another's? I might as well shut my incantations up, and allow things to take their natural course.' So she locked up her books in her cupboard and only used her wand as a walking cane.

When the Princess Angelica was born, her parents did not ask the Fairy Blackstick to the christening party and gave orders to their porter to

refuse her if she called. This porter's name was Gruffanuff, and he had been selected by their Royal Highnesses because he was a tall fierce man, with a rudeness that frightened people away.

When the Fairy Blackstick called upon the prince and princess, Gruffanuff made the most vulgar sign as he started to slam the door in the fairy's face! "Get away, Blackstick!" said he. "I tell you, Master and Missis ain't at home to you."

But the fairy, with her wand, prevented the door being shut, and Gruffanuff came out again in a fury, asking the fairy 'whether she thought he was going to stay at that there door all day?'

"You are going to stay at that door all day and night, for many a long year," the fairy said.

Gruffanuff, coming out of the door, burst out laughing, and cried, "Ha, ha! This is a good un! Let me down —O—o!" and then he was dumb!

The Fairy Blackstick

For, as the fairy waved her wand over
him, he felt himself rising off the ground,
and fluttering up against the door, and then
he was pinned to the door. He felt cold, as if
he were turning into metal.

He was turned into metal! He was neither
more nor less than a knocker! And there he was,
nailed to the door in the blazing summer day, till
he burned almost red-hot, and there he was,
nailed to the door all the bitter winter nights, till his
brass nose was dropping with icicles. And the
postman came and rapped at him, and the boy
with a letter came and hit him up against the door.

And that evening, when the king and queen
came home from a walk, the king said, "Hello, my
dear! You have had a new knocker put on the
door. Why, it's rather like our porter in the face!
What has become of that lazy man?" And the

housemaid came and scrubbed his nose with sandpaper, and once, some larking young men tried to wrench him off, and put him to the most excruciating agony with a screwdriver. And then the queen had a fancy to have the colour of the door altered, and the painters dabbed him over the mouth and eyes, and nearly choked him, as they painted him pea-green.

As for his wife, she did not miss him, and when the prince and princess chose to become king and queen, they left their old house, and nobody thought of the porter any more.